Dedication

Dedicated to my wonderful Dad,

Ben Smedley.

A beautiful, loving soul.

JOHN

He is a wise man in tune with nature. All of his life he has lived in this ancient woodland, he is the last of its protectors. For centuries his family have lived on this land, you could say owned the land, but John knows that although he has the deeds for this land he does not own it. The land cannot be owned by man. John knows he is a part of the land, that he is privileged to be a part of this special place. He hears when the woods speak to him; they guide him and they energise him. They led him long ago to the special places that only he is allowed to go. No other human has seen them, yet he never feels alone. He knows he is watched and at times he has glimpsed those watching him. They live alongside him and work with him, they laugh with him too. The energies of the woodland protect them.

John has always been in tune with the woods, he feels the love there, and this, together with the unconditional love of his parents, is reflected in the gentle giant of the man. His father was an expert woodsman and passed all of his skills on to John. His mother would gather the herbs and wild flowers, she knew them all and their healing properties. She too passed her skills and knowledge on to John. John is the sum of all the experience of his ancestors. All knowledge has been passed down the many generations, it is in the fabric of the building of his home, in the land they had tilled for their food and in the woods of which they had all taken turns being the guardians. Over time they had expanded their 'ownership' of land and so it too was protected by them. Until in the end the whole valley was protected.

His home was simple and basic - not quite so basic now, as John had modern technology and electricity - but so used was he to going to bed and rising with the sun that he rarely used it. His heating was with wood, he cooked with a wood-burning stove and even his work he did the ancient traditional way. At night he would sit by the light of the fire and let the peace wash over him. It was at these times he would be guided; solutions would be given and he had learned to act on them. He was at one with his environment.

John worked with wood, oh yes he protected the forest, he coppiced to give him the wood for his fuel, the wood for his fences and the charcoal. But what he loved most of all was to walk the woodland for the gifts from the trees: the fallen branches and old stumps. These he would take back to his workshop and smooth them until they became so tactile that once touched it was hard to let them go. John would do it all by hand, he rubbed them down, never altering their shape. The beauty of the contours of each piece was enhanced by his touch. His gift was to become one with the wood, and as he worked to bring out the beauty of each piece, so too would his love be poured into the wood itself. The energy of each piece was almost palpable, they were spiritual pieces, the joining together of two entities, man and nature. They could not become ornaments, for those who owned them could not resist touching them. They did not realise that they did this, but did so nonetheless, particularly at times when they needed the love that was infused into the wood. It was as though a light was being passed that would light up the world. Each light healing the pain of those who touched it. Giving unconditional love and energy to each individual. And each piece was destined for a particular person. No matter who purchased it, it always found its way home to the person it was destined to help. Some pieces, once their work was done, would be passed on to another. Or they would simply disappear, only to be found by the next person destined to own it. He knew little of this, only that he loved the work he did and each piece he worked with; he knew a part of him was woven in with the wood, but not of the effect each piece had on others. This was his work, his work with this ancient woodland; both, between them, protected the forest and helped man.

As he worked the wood John would remember his parents and the old family story they would tell him; a myth. Little did he know that this story was a message passed to him from the beginning, a message that each generation had memorised and passed down to their children. A message which, over time, became myth and then simply a story. A message never forgotten even as it became a story. In the remembering he lost himself in the task as though in a trance. Sometimes hours would pass when to him it seemed like only minutes. At first he would wonder where his mind had drifted off to but he came to accept it, knowing little of the wondrous things that were happening to him and the wood he was so lovingly working with.

It was at these times that the wood, through John, was infused with what was needed for the person it was destined for. To John it was simply a form of meditation, doing what he loved most.

SARAH

Today she had been given the diagnosis; it was cancer. She had left it too late to consult a doctor and it had spread. 12 months. So little time. She had wanted to complete her research and had postponed returning home. She had done what she always did, she had put her work first. Not her career but her work. She was a botanist and conservationist. Her life had been to protect the earth, to show the different peoples of the earth ways they could live at one with their environment. There was no need to cut down the great ancient forests to earn their living. They earned so little. Often they were forcibly removed from their land to enable the large land owners and the huge conglomerates to expand and get rich at the expense of not only the earth but the people who had lived off the land for generations. Her work was her passion. It was a passion that had cost her so much and now...

She stood there at the reception almost in a daze. Inside she was screaming when others were laughing. Couldn't they see her pain, could they not feel it? How could they possibly laugh when her world was falling apart. 'Pull yourself together' she told herself. She did what she did best; she smothered her own needs and acted out a role with which she could face the world. Even now, with this devastating news she could not get in contact with herself. She smiled to herself, now I have two secrets. The thought of them both brought pain.

The speeches were starting, her son stepped forward, he had inherited his father's business. A business the complete antithesis of her work, how had it happened? She had met Jack at university out in California.

They shared the same dreams, they wanted the world to be a better place. They had protested at the Vietnam war and had fallen in love. Upon getting her doctorate they married. They stayed in California and she moved into conservation work, they were happy. Being a chemist he went to work for a chemical company. Then a year after their marriage she went on a week's course in the north. It was a beautiful place, the course covered work she had done before so she started skipping the lectures. It was then she met him.

She had put on her walking boots, packed a lunch and had decided to walk up the mountain side and onto a section of forest that seemed to be calling her. It was in this forest of tall redwoods that they met. They were on the same pathway going in opposite directions. She looked up to say hi and it happened. She looked into his eyes and there was instant recognition. So powerful was the recognition that she was stopped in her tracks and so was he. It was like coming home, they had found each other. Neither understood what was happening to them but they knew it was something special. They were wary at first, but as they talked it was as though they had known each other all of their lives. In fact it had been lifetimes. Little did they know but they were destined to find each other in each of the lifetimes they shared. He had just finished his doctorate and was taking a year to walk the Rockies before taking up a job with Natural Resources Canada. His love was trees.

As they talked they began to understand the bond between them. A great love that was centuries old and there in that ancient forest they made love. It was not a gentle lovemaking. They were hungry for each other. Instinctively each knew the other's needs. His touch was electrifying and their passion overwhelming. They made love and satiated their desire of each other. Afterwards he led her to a clearing of spring mountain flowers. He lifted her in his powerful arms and laid her down and there, amongst the beauty and the heady perfume of the flowers, they explored each other's bodies and again ignited their passion. They made love, slowly at first, revelling in the joy of each other; a remembering. Their bodies moving as one, their kisses, gentle at first, soon became all consuming as their passion once again led them forward. Instinctively each knew what the other desired, each gave themselves to the other, moving as one, until they reached an ecstasy that transported them beyond themselves and united them with all that is; they became their spirit.

They were together for four days. They made love. They talked, they talked of their plans to be together. He would take her back to Canada but it was not to be. At the end of the four days it was time for her to return home. She could not hurt her husband. It was so strange loving two men in such different ways. She too had her work, work that she thought vital in the world of conservation. Yet she loved this man with all of her being, they understood that their love was as old as time. That the four days was a gift. That for them to be together others would be hurt and neither could inflict the pain. She had met her soul mate and the parting was as though she were being torn in two. She never again felt complete. Always there was something missing. He was missing. At times she would think of him and tears of longing for him would gently fall. Yet she lived a happy life with her husband, for a while.

Her husband had always been ambitious and they had planned to delay having a family until he was established, but it was not to be and their son was born. He spent little time with him, he was too busy with his career. Five years later they had a daughter and she became the apple of his eye. By then he had set up his own business and he spent even more hours working. They became quite wealthy. As his children got older he had more time for them, but always her son was wary of him. He had wanted his father's love but it was conditional love he received. He was not to disturb him in his study. If he did, his father would lose his temper with him. He became nervous around him, but still looked for his approval and love. Yet his sister could do no wrong; only for her the unconditional love. When they were old enough they went to boarding school. Sarah thought this was best for them, she had spent months vetting the prospective schools. She wanted them to be able to relax and be themselves. She hated parting from them, but she saw it as the only way other than divorce. She had broached the subject once and he had quietly told her it was out of the question, there had been menace in his eyes. When had he changed she wondered? He threatened to keep the children, so she stayed. She knew she could not inflict that pain on her children, especially her son. He was special to her, she felt a closeness to him. To her, her son was a gift of love.

With the children away at school she devoted more time to her work. She became a renowned expert in conservation. She spent months in the South American rainforest, not only on conservation work, but also studying the plant life. Working with the native peoples, she learned of the uses for the plants and trees; of the many benefits this plant life had for man. At times she was away from home when her children had returned for their school holidays, such was the importance of her work. Ironic really, she thought now: I did to them what my husband had done to them. Ironic too that she and her husband had ended up on opposite sides.

With the onset of genetic engineering her husband had been on a mission, he recognised that with the ever-expanding world population, he who controls the food would make the biggest profits. He had set up his biotech business and was now buying up seed companies. He became a huge conglomerate. In the undeveloped world he preyed on small farmers persuading them to buy his genetically modified seeds. He sold them at especially cheap prices. The farmers believed what his representatives told them. The seeds would be drought resistant and herbicide resistant. Their yields would be double what they were getting from their old seed. Their tradition had been to save some of the best seed from each harvest for the following year's planting. But with buying the genetic seed this was not possible. If seed was saved for the following years' planting the biotech company would sue the farmer. The company claimed ownership of the seed. With no seed the farmers were forced to return to his biotech company to buy more seed. Once reliant on the seed company the prices were increased. The farmers found the yields were lower than promised, even with the expensive fertilisers they also needed to purchase from the company. Yes, she and her husband were on opposite sides of the fence and they grew even further apart.

As she spent more and more of her time on her work her husband's influence grew over his son and in time this gentle boy, who so longed for his father's approval, started to become like his father. In doing so he became hard. To get attention from his father he had to change who he was. Over the years this gentle boy, in tune with nature, turned against it. He became his father, but even more so. She saw his struggle, even now. He was still that gentle creature she had nurtured in his early years, but in his struggle to obtain his father's attention and love he had turned himself into his father. His inner battle was sometimes too much to bear. His temper was renowned, he had little patience for the mistakes of others. He became his father's right hand man. He was being moulded to take over the company one day. He would do so with aggression.

Then five years ago her husband had collapsed and died from a heart attack. She had felt sad at his passing, remembering their early happy lives together. But at the same time it was a relief. Her son had only been 25 and he took over the company. It grew and became even more powerful. But she didn't like what he was turning into.

Her daughter had left home as soon as she could and now lived in the East in New York. She had gone as far away as possible. 'I have spent years trying to save the planet and the peoples on it and in doing so I have neglected my family. So much damage'. Was it too late?

She left the reception. She needed fresh air, time to think, time to be alone. She found herself standing in front of a gallery window. She felt compelled to go inside. There were some beautiful works of art, but what drew her attention was a piece of polished wood. It was very small, small enough to fit into the palm of her hand. Although it clearly stated that the works of art should not be touched she felt compelled to pick it up. It was as though the wood spoke to her. She felt the smoothness of it, yet it was something more than this tactile feeling; she was connected to it, a belonging, a coming home. The feeling was familiar, she had felt it before but it was deep in her memory and she couldn't quite grasp it. The gallery owner approached her and saw what she was holding. He told her it was by a Canadian artist by the name of John, simply John. Her memory came to the surface, she remembered him, the meeting in the forest, the gifted four days. Could it be the same John? But he wasn't an artist, he was going to work for Natural Resources Canada, it couldn't be, it just couldn't be. So she dismissed the thought but she did buy the piece. She didn't let it go. All the time she held it she felt at peace. Even the pain of the diagnosis was eased. All that week she kept her diagnosis to herself. She walked, she slept, it was all a dream she said to herself. It was difficult to come to terms with it all. And all the time she held the piece of wood. She would dream of

John, she awoke at times calling his name, but he wasn't there.

She felt as though she were in a trance and slowly as the week passed she came out of it. She had clarity of what was happening to her and what she must do. John was at the centre. She had walked away from him; he who was so much a part of her, they were two halves of the one. Theirs was not a symbiotic relationship but one of a true meeting of souls. It was as if they shared the same body, had the same thoughts yet at the same time they were themselves. Neither asked anything of the other, it was a love that made no demands and took nothing from the other. Yet each received so much from the other because it was given and given in love; two souls finding each other. There were no secrets; there was no pretense; it was as if all the worldly desires and possessions had fallen aside. What was left was their pure essence and with this there was a knowing. A knowing of such purity and of such love, it was as though they needed nothing other than the essence they shared. 'It is time, at last...'

She returned to the gallery and enquired about the artist who had crafted her wood that she still held in her hand. He knew little other than the area of Canada where he lived. It was a start. She could feel a warm glow of excitement starting to grow within her; yes, she knew that what she was doing was the right action. It was then that she noticed another crafted piece of wood and she knew it too was by John, even before she touched it and felt his essence. It was larger than the one she held in her hand and it held a beauty that could not be resisted. It had to be touched, its contours and colours were almost mesmeric to her and she knew where it belonged and with whom. She bought it. Then she returned home. She retired from her work. She knew it would go on and that there were many like her who were dedicated to the protection of the earth. She had helped lead the way, she had done what she was meant to do and it was time for her to move on. She couldn't really believe that she could walk away from her work so easily. It had been her passion, her motivation for so long. It was finished; she had a knowing, yes a knowing - it was the only way she could describe it; a knowing that what she was about to do was what she was here to do. All that had gone before had been leading her to this point. Yes, it is time, at last...

She called James, her son, and invited him to dinner; he who was always so busy, so wrapped up in the company, but tonight he was free. Yes, it is time. She told him she had resigned, that she was going on a long trip to Canada on a walking holiday and would be out of contact for some time. He had looked at her for a while without speaking. His mother going on a holiday? Actually resigning from the work she put even before her family? Yet she had an inner glow about her, something he had never seen in her before. It brought an unexpected smile to his hardened features. His mother, on seeing this, was reminded of the gentle child he had once been and she knew that he was still in there, deep inside her son, watching over him until her son returned. James accepted what she was doing and wished her well on her holiday. They had a pleasant evening, one that for once had no tension, that old connection was still there. She slept so much better that night; it was as though John was watching over her.

The following day she went to the airport to fly to New York. On the way she dropped into her son's office. With her she took the crafted wood she had purchased yesterday. Her son was away at a meeting and so she placed it on his desk with a note simply saying that this was a gift of love from her. With a smile she left and went on her way.

In New York she went to see her daughter, to tell her too that she was going on an extended walking holiday. This daughter who was so special to her. She had been the oh so obvious favourite of her husband, no restrictions on his time for her, such different treatment from that of her son. Her daughter had grown up feeling loved by both parents, she had never looked for her father's love, her father's time, for he had given it freely. Not for her the anger of his being disturbed, not for her standing on the sidelines waiting to be invited into the fun. It was as she got older, in her teenage years that she started to see the difference in her father's attitude to his two children. Always she had been unconditionally loved by all in her family. Even her brother, so cruelly treated by his father, had always given her love, always was there for her, always supported her in all that she did. It was he who taught her so many things to do with nature, he who showed her his love of everything to do with nature. It was only as she began to see the treatment her brother received from his father that she looked back and saw the differing treatments of the brother and sister. It was then that beautiful child became angry at her brother's treatment. She became angry with everyone. Only her mother understood, but it was her mother she was most angry with so her mother had to keep quiet. She knew that she could say nothing to her daughter, that she must be left to work through the anger herself, all she could do was love her, but even this was rejected. But then she too had also been struggling with her own inner demons. Now her demons had been laid to rest and she knew it was time. Time to lay to rest the anger of her daughter.

The years spent in New York had mellowed her daughter, she had worked through her anger. They had never lost touch; underneath her demons and her daughter's anger, there was still that special relationship they had always had; each knew that, but neither could return to it. But now the years of skirting around each other had passed, of one being angry and the other wanting to please and wanting her child to return. They didn't speak of the past for each recognised the pain, suffering and work each had endured to get them to where they were today. She let her daughter go, she knew her daughter was strong, that she had her own life to lead and she had a good life in New York. She saw that at last the anger was gone, that this self-assured young woman was confident in herself. She knew what she wanted, she knew where she was going, but she would do it gently and with love; her daughter had returned. Both mother and daughter could now go their separate ways, each had made peace with each other. It was as though lifetimes of difficulties in their relationships had been resolved, that they had at last worked through what they were here to do. They each found peace together. 'It is time'.

She arrived in Canada with no other information than the gallery address that she had been given as the supplier to the gallery back home. Still it was a good start. She felt so optimistic. Again she had that knowing that she would find him, that everything she was doing was right. That the time was right, that the time is now.

Her path lay before her and she was being shown the way. It was as though she was being taken by the hand by a very gentle, old soul and was being guided. She had done all she could do in her old life. Yes, it was her old life, and now she was on the edge of a new beginning. All that had gone before was the foundation she had laid down to build this new beginning. She was going into the unknown. It was like jumping off a cliff. She knew that in jumping there was no danger, as the act of jumping was a leap of faith. Faith that she was at last on the last leg of her path, a path she was born to. She knew now that what she was going to do was destined to be. She didn't know what it was but she knew the dinner with her son, the crafted wood she had left him and the days with her daughter were the beginning of this final leg. She had completed her old life, she could do no more for either her son or her daughter. They had chosen their paths; she must step off their paths and, in the time she had left, follow her own. Now was her time. Yes, it was time and it felt so very good.

Oh the joy of the adventure, for that is surely what this is. On arrival she booked into a hotel; she was travelling very light, all she wanted was in a small backpack. It felt good to be free of the trappings of wealth. What need had she of that great house in which she just rattled around? Yes, they were trappings. The organising of running such a house took her energy. It had been the house her husband had acquired as a status symbol. Not a home just a house. Yes, she would sell it on her return. Why wait? She picked up the phone, spoke to her lawyer and asked him to arrange to sell it. There, that was done. 'Well,' she thought to herself, 'if I'm on this path and I like this path, then allow me let go of the old with grace. That house will make a perfect family home, it needs a family; it longs for a family. That is what it was built for.' She liked this new way of thinking; a change to the old material way she had lived without realising it. The building she had lived in - built originally with love by a man for his beloved wife and family - had felt a lonely place. It was a lonely building, it was meant for noise and laughter and the love of a loving family. Time to let it too get back on its path. Yes, life was getting better.

The following morning she found the gallery. She felt the tingling of excitement and anticipation. She knew she was going to find him. She had thought no further than that. She had a goal and the goal was simply to find him. Strange that her scientific mind thought nothing beyond this. Indeed there was nothing to think beyond the immediate future. Wasn't this why she was leaving behind everything that was so familiar, everything that made her feel safe? Oh how we hang on to the familiar to feel safe, when in fact we are stunting our growth, blocking our path. Yes, jumping off a cliff was exciting; she had not felt this alive for such a long time, not since those four days they had been given.

Such a wonderful gift. Why had they never exchanged surnames, just their first names? They had talked so much - of their plans and their lives; they knew so much of each other, so much about their respective pasts, yet never their surnames. Was that part of this plan? Yes, it did seem to her that she was part of a plan, a vast all-encompassing plan, and she had no say in where it was directing her. She felt as though she had been following the plan all of her life and that it had led her to this point. Oh yes, she had no doubt she would find him. No, she didn't know his name. She believed he was working for Natural Resources Canada, so how could he have produced these sensitive pieces of wood? Yet she felt his essence in the two pieces she had come into contact with. She was on a journey of faith. She knew she would find him. She walked into the gallery.

More beautifully crafted pieces of wood. She knew that they, like the pieces she had purchased, had not been cut or damaged in any way. Each piece was as it was in nature; each piece retained its own essence; each piece was respected for what it was. There was no pressure or imposing of his will on the wood. He had simply and lovingly smoothed the wood and in doing so he had brought forth its inner beauty. An inner beauty which he could see before the smoothing of it, so why smooth it at all? It was a partnership between the man and the wood. The smoothing was part of the greater plan.

It was too soon for her to realise the meaning of his smoothing of the wood. Too soon for her to realise that with both the man and the wood working together they each gave their energy and essence to those who came into contact with each piece. No knowledge yet of the destiny of each piece. No knowledge that each piece was there and chosen for a specific purpose.

This knowledge was beyond her imagination, this knowledge was from a realm that was not within the boundaries of human knowledge. Yet it guided her on her path of life, it was with her constantly, it surrounded her in love, just at it did for all peoples. She would learn to connect to this unconditional love. She would realise that the human condition and its attachment to things and people simply blocked out this love. This attachment was a searching for what was there for each of us. This love given freely by the Universe, God or whatever you may call it, is there for all. We simply blind ourselves to it. Yes she would learn, she was learning; the act of walking into the gallery was a certain sign of it.

She touched the wood and again felt his essence, the peace flowed through her, she could almost see him in the process of smoothing this piece. The gallery owner asked if he could help. She explained that she was trying to find the maker of the wood pieces and was surprised by the answer. He didn't know his address or even his surname, the man came in periodically with more pieces and would leave them with him. As each piece was sold he simply transferred the funds for each piece to the account number he had given him. It had been that way for years. Years of increasing demand for the pieces and with that, the increasing wealth for both the artist and the gallery owner. Yet he knew little of him other that that he was a good man and he felt protective of the craftsman's privacy.

It had started as an almost casual agreement. He had walked into the gallery one day many years ago with several pieces of his work, and asked the owner if he was interested in buying them. The owner had agreed to take the pieces. He liked the artist immediately, he had a presence about him. He was a man who knew himself, was confident in himself yet made no demands on others, he was comfortable with who he was. He had left the pieces and the account number and gone. The pieces had sold quickly. Over time he began to sell to other galleries in the large cities, from this the orders came from other cities around the world. Commissions were out of the question for each piece was as nature intended it. This seemed to intensify the interest and within a few years demand had outstripped supply, with the purchase price sometimes being many thousands of dollars for each piece. Yet the artist never changed; he was constant, the money was not important to him. He would arrive in the same ancient pick up truck - oh, it had certainly lived; how he kept it going for so long he just never knew, but keep going it did. Each piece of wood was lovingly wrapped for the journey and carefully secured in the rear of the pickup. He looked forward to each delivery. It was as though the forest took over his gallery, it wasn't the amount of pieces but the energy of them. It wasn't just invigorating, it brought balance and peace to him too.

He came to realise the effect the man and his work had on him over the years. He was ambitious when he opened his shop, he had visions of wealth, travel and of having a chain of his shops. But it seems that almost from the day John walked into his shop the ambitions began to fade. Oh yes, John had brought him wealth, but even before this he started to be content with where he was. He started to appreciate this small town, it was no longer an ignorant backwater to him. He saw what his ambition had blinded him to, the love that was here. The people supported each other. They weren't ignorant. But what is ignorance? He had been to college, yet those in this town who hadn't, had a knowledge that books could not give you. It was a poor community and the richer for it. They could not afford the luxury items, yet they had so much more. They had community. They looked after each other. They knew the seasons, they knew how to live with nature and each other. When someone was sick they were looked after. They respected the old and cared for them. Yet it wasn't claustrophobic, each person was respected for who they were. Over time he had ceased to resent being here. Rather, he resented going away from the place. Oh, with the increasing demand for John's work and the wealth it gave him he was able to travel, yet as time went by he yearned more to return. He, too, became more and more comfortable with who he was.

Money stopped being the god he had made it. Yes, he had plenty of money, but he used little of it. He had put the money into the needs of the town, so each person had benefited from his wealth and he did it in a way that didn't belittle anyone; neither did it make him the great benefactor. He was not above anyone else, he had learned that each person contributed in their own right. That each contribution was equally important, no matter who they were or what the contribution. That each made the whole and without each there could be no whole. Yes, it was a good place to be and he thanked John for being able to realise this. In fact he always made sure there was at least one piece of John's work left at the gallery, simply because it felt good having it there.

He had become quite protective of John over the years. Others had wanted to meet him but he gave them no information. Yet this woman was different. There was something familiar about her and he realised that she had the same qualities as John. He wanted to help her. He explained that John would just appear with his next batch of work; there was no pattern to his deliveries, though he hadn't been for some time. She gave him her mobile number and asked him to call her should John arrive. She was staying at the local hotel and would stay there until she heard from him. With that she left the shop.

She had felt so sure she would find him. She felt devastated. She wanted so much to see him. She had been certain that he would be there; that she would be given his name and address; that she would go to him and that it would be as before. 'Fantasies', she told herself. She had been like a school girl with her first love. She felt the tears in her eyes, she needed to walk and she did. She was angry with herself, she walked blindly on.

It was a small town and she was soon out into the countryside.

She could see the mountains in the distance, yet not so distant, it was as if she could reach out and touch them. So majestic, they seemed unreal. Were they real or just cardboard cut-outs? Their beauty was too much to take in, too unbelievable. Their sheer size and power overwhelmed her. Mountains always did this. She loved them, felt a part of them and wondered at their majesty. Were they themselves alive and moving in their worlds? From her perspective they were still, or was it that she was moving at such a speed that they appeared still? Was she just an insignificant speck of dust in the world of the mountains? If they could communicate, what could they tell her, what had they seen? Always they brought these questions, this wonder. And in being here amongst the trees and the mountains she felt her peace return, the anger abated. Yes, she was disappointed at not knowing where to find him, but she had over the past days woven fantasies about finding him. She had been brought back to reality with the disappointment of coming this far and not being able to complete her fantasy. She would find him, she had felt him calling her. He would find her.

He had woken suddenly from a deep sleep. Someone was calling his name. He had been dreaming. He lay there trying to recall the dream. It had happened last night and the night before, but he couldn't remember. As hard as he tried it was impossible. It had haunted him through the day, yet he couldn't quite grasp it. He lay there in the dark listening to the night sounds around the cottage. There it was again, he could see it but not quite grasp it, yet it felt so familiar, something from the past, something he had buried so deep within himself that he had forgotten it, such was the pain it brought him. Better to bury it than to live with that pain. A pain so deep it tore him in two. A longing, a searching, all buried. He drifted into a dreamless sleep.

The following day he felt listless, no work today, he would walk in the forest and the forest guided him to where he needed to go; to where it would begin the ending.

He walked for hours until he came to the clearing, the glade, the centre of the reason for this forest, the centre of the story, the centre of the reason for his being. Immediately he felt at peace, gone was this grasping of what he could not remember, the frustration of the recognition he simply could not recognise. Strange to see it in his mind's eye so clearly yet he could not grasp it, so familiar was it that it disappeared when he tried to focus on it. But now he felt the familiar peace this place gave him. It seemed as though he was always drawn here when troubled. He would try to find it at other times but it always eluded him. The familiar paths would lead him elsewhere, but today they led him to this beautiful place. A place of such beauty. The circle of the large, ancient trees which seemed to speak to him. They had the knowledge of the ancients. He knew this, but not how he knew it. It was as though he was at one with this place. It gave him solace and fed him, gave him strength and clarity. Its stillness also gave him his peace.

So often in the past, at troubled times, he had found himself here, often not knowing how he had arrived or what he was doing before he had walked here. Always at these times his mind had cleared and the answers had come to him. Strange that he had never recognised this before. Something, he felt, no, knew with certainty, was about to happen. Something his life had been leading him to. He felt a connection to all who had protected this land before him, his ancestors, the ancient ones, it was here that it would happen. Where had that thought come from? He couldn't say, yet he knew he was right, he knew this place had always given him the answers, that this sacred place - yes it was a sacred place - had brought him here to give him a gift. But this gift was not the ending, it was the beginning of the end. An end to all that had gone before.

The ancients had moved here many centuries before. The story his parents had told him was of a tribe of people who had lived at peace and in harmony with nature. All nature had been honoured. Animals had not been killed for sport, only for survival: for food, clothes and housing. Each animal had not been hunted, it had presented itself at the right time, when needed. It had lived its life and had completed its task on this earth. When it was ready it would die and move on, but if needed it would present itself to support those in need of its sustenance. In doing so it would be thanked for its sacrifice and honoured. And it too would live on in those who ate it, wore its skin as clothing and lived under its skin as protection. Its knowledge would be passed on and in so doing the respect of man and animal would grow. Their shared lives were entwined for ever. It was as though the two stems of man and animal had fused together, each unable and unwilling to separate, yet each living independently of the other. Their love of the other sustaining them.

The story his parents had told him was that of a white buffalo who had spoken to the holy one and told of the future. That a group of men would come and destroy all before them. That nothing could be saved and that the ancients must leave that place of abundance and travel north. That in the north there was a place waiting for them that would, with their help, be protected for the good of mother earth and the people who lived on and in harmony with her. They would take an oath to protect this land and the secret it would hold. They would not know the secret, only that within the forest was a sacred place which none other than those who were to follow would enter to fulfill the destiny of their people. The story recounted how the wisdom of their people would be passed from generation to generation, that all their knowledge and knowing would be within those who were to come.

John had been told of this story and of the painful journey his people made to this land, of the many obstacles they had overcome and in overcoming them how they had learnt each lesson these obstacles had given them. That they had always held true to the belief and knowledge that their journey was a gift to them and to all who would follow. That at each stage of their journey - for they knew nothing other than they had to travel north - they were given signs of which direction to go. They came across land that would have supported them, but over time each of the ancients learned of their connectivity with nature, with mother earth, and they knew that this was not the land they were here to protect and so they moved ever further north. North, to what is now Canada, north to this valley, this valley that not only sustained their bodies but also their spirit.

The ancients had known immediately that this was the place and they had settled. They worked with nature to nurture not only the valley but also themselves. They were the guardians of this land, a land of such abundance, beauty and peace. It had been a journey of faith and of love. There had been heartache and loss on their journey, yet each had known that this was what they were here to do. The loss of those on the journey was seen as those completing their purpose on earth and returning home. The loss was to those left behind, even with the knowledge that those who died had returned home and were joyous. Yet those who had gone before were never forgotten, they were woven into what had become the story. The story which John had been told by his parents, in particular his mother. Until they too had returned home and it was for John to mourn them and his loss.

Here he was, the last of his people. He had often thought of the story, for that is what he believed it to be: a story. He could never understand his mother's insistence that he pass on the story to his own children when the time was right. At her passing she had again made him promise to pass on the story of the ancients to his own children. He could see her anxiety and he had promised and with that promise she was at peace and she left him to make her journey home. Was it she who had been calling him? He who, he believed, was the last of his people. The answer was immediate. No. 'Then who?', he asked.

Then he saw her: the journey he was on so many years ago, walking the Rockies. The path on which they had met, the instant recognition they had for each other, their lovemaking, their passion for each other, their fulfillment. The knowing that they were twin souls and the four days of absolute bliss. He remembered their plans and their parting. A parting which had torn him in two, his soul aching for her. The pain of the parting he had buried so long ago, now surfaced and washed over him, he was drowning in it. He could feel it tearing through his body, it was as if he had returned to that time. A time of such hopes, a job he had wanted and would be starting at the end of his trekking through the Rockies, yet it was not to be. He had had a breakdown and had wandered this forest for weeks, or was it months, he didn't know. He had returned home unable to say what was happening to him. His parents had seen that he needed only their love and that they should leave him to heal. That time, their love and the forest would help him.

It was then that he had first found this clearing, this glade, this place that gave him such peace. He had come here many times in the following months. Over time he had buried the memory of those four days and the pain that followed, but in burying it he had only pushed it deep down inside him. It had been stored in the back of that cupboard he never opened, but it had not gone away, it had waited for him, for a time when he was ready. Was he ready now? He didn't know, he felt only the pain. He fell to the ground and lay there, curled up trying to ease the pain of her loss, of their parting. He knew that she too had felt this same pain. He relived those four days again and the pain eased until he fell into a deep sleep.

He felt disoriented, where was he? The memory of yesterday returned, yet the pain didn't. Why? And why was he still there in the glade? Dawn was just breaking and he felt its peace wash over him. He lay there in the sweetness of the meadow flowers, still untouched by the rising sun and he remembered the dream of last night. Or was it a dream? He had seen his hopes as a young man fresh from university, of the job he had wanted, waiting for him. He had so wanted to move away from this valley, yet it was to the valley he returned to heal. He had blocked out all of the pain of parting and in doing so he had blocked out the gift of the four days. Yes, he remembered the dream now; it had shown him the four days was a gift, that it should not be wasted; everything had a purpose. He thought of her again, of those four days, their dreams of being together and then her telling him that she must return home. That she loved the man waiting for her and could not hurt him. She had known then that those four days had been a gift, a gift to hold in their hearts. Not the pain of parting, but the memory of a love which transcended time itself. Yes, from the dream he also remembered that they had been together before, several times, in other lifetimes. Theirs was, is, a love of twin souls. The instant recognition, the knowing of a connection so powerful, yet of not knowing. Neither had understood their history, yet they had come together as though they had never been parted. The joy of finding each other; they had come together to complete something left undone. What, he wondered, was it? Had they completed it? 'Not yet', came the thought? 'It is time.'.

He didn't understand where the thoughts had come from. Yet it didn't seem to matter, not in this place of such beauty and peace. He sat up. 'It is time' - what did that mean?

In front of him was a flower; it hadn't yet opened for the day and he sat and watched it. The day was warming and with it the flower began to unfurl. Its petals held tight in the cold, protecting its inner core. As the dawning of the day progressed so too did the flower. Gently, slowly, the petals once again opened to the new day. He watched with wonder as they released themselves from each other, the guardians of their core, and as they unfurled they revealed its inner beauty, a beauty he had never seen before. He had never looked; he who was so in tune with this valley had never looked into the heart of the flowers themselves. He was being given another gift - what was this unfurling beauty showing him? What was he seeing in this mirror before him? Then he knew, he knew so clearly. He had buried their love and joy deep within him, buried so deep that he had forgotten it. It was the heart of him that he had folded the petals around and had kept it locked away all these years. Yet in locking his heart away he had locked himself away. Oh, he had enjoyed his life, the love of this valley, his being in tune with it. But now it was different.

The petals had unfolded, he had set his heart free. He knew that he had had help last night. That his dream wasn't a dream, it was something he had lived, he had been shown that to lock his heart away had been to block his path. Yes there had been pain, such pain it was unbearable at times. He had been taken back to those days, weeks and months after she had left him. Months of wandering the valley, months of not being able to explain to his parents. He had felt again their unconditional love; not questioning him, but letting him find a place within himself that would enable him to move forward. He saw too that they knew the reason for his grief, for grief is what it was, a loss. He saw himself calling her name in his sleep and his parents hearing him. Yet they never told him, they carried on their lives and in doing so it gave him the grounding he needed. He was able to come to terms with all he had lost. Only now did he realise he had not, until today, come to terms with it. Now he knew they had been given this gift, he wanted to follow her, to take her away from the man she had married; he couldn't understand how a woman could love two men, yet in different ways, but love them both she did. One who knew of the other, the other who knew nothing of him. Yes, he understood now and with the understanding came the peace. His heart was released, he remembered the joy of their being together and accepted the gift and in doing so he opened his heart again. And he knew that it was all for a reason, a reason he didn't know. 'But you will. It is time'. There, it had happened again, the thought. Not his thought, but what was it? He felt rather than heard the chuckle, yet he heard 'Welcome back'. He looked around, no-one there, he was alone. But he knew he wasn't.

He asked if there was anybody there and he was told they were there. They had always been there and they had been waiting for him; for it was time. Time for what, he didn't understand. 'You have unlocked your heart. It is time.'

It is time. He knew what was in his thoughts was right but he didn't understand how the thoughts got there, from where did they come?

'Live from your heart not from your head. See the world from your heart. Look at the world with closed eyes, with your heart, your feelings. Then you will begin to understand the meaning of life. All life, in its entirety. We are here, we have always been here, waiting for you, watching over you. Waiting to work with you to complete your work'. He knew then that the question he had often asked himself had been answered. Yes, he was here for a purpose . Oh, he didn't know what the purpose was, but it didn't matter. He knew, yes knew, he had a knowing that it had all begun with those four days. What it was he didn't know, and he didn't need to know, yet. The time will come and it will be soon. There it was again, 'It is time'. He knew there was nothing he could do only to stay attuned as he was at this moment. They, whoever they were, had brought him here to this place, he knew this; they had given him his heart back last night, he knew this; they had shown him the path he must follow and what he must do next and he knew they were right. He felt a great love around and within him. It had always been there, it wasn't just here in the valley, but everywhere. Not just for him but for all mankind, all sentient beings.

He saw that people spent so much time looking outside of themselves for the answers, reading books, learning, even simply shopping, always driven to find the answers, always ready to 'blame' someone or something else. Never looking at themselves and in doing so people became more and more dissatisfied, burying deeper what needed most to be addressed. Never looking within. Blocking themselves from moving forward to this state of - what could it be called? - this feeling he was feeling. Bliss? Yes, bliss. Gone was his loneliness, gone was the grief. Here was a love that was so enveloping that he felt wrapped in it.

Yet it didn't smother him. He had his free will, but this is where he wanted to be. He knew this was his next chapter. This was where his life had been bringing him. This was where they had been leading him. He felt liberated, free, full of love and joy; it was exhilarating. And there it was; the knowing, the knowing that he would find her again. The joy spread across his face. It is time.

He left the glade and was led to the lake. This place too, he felt, was sacred. He stripped and dived into the cold water. He felt a warm glow in this water. He dived down and looked up. He could see the sun dancing on the surface, the blue green of the water enveloped him, he merged with it. It cleansed him, it baptised him. This is a new life. This is what he is here to do. All would be revealed to him. He dedicated himself to this work and what lay ahead. He broke the surface and entered his new world.

JAMES

James walked into his office, closed the door and just stood there. It had happened again, no thrill at the kill. He had just completed another hostile take over. This is what gave his adrenaline a charge, what motivated him, his ambition, yet there was nothing. He who was always in charge of every aspect of his life, who took no advice from anyone, hesitated. He simply stood there and looked around his office. It was plush, luxurious, a statement of his success and great wealth. He could make people bow to his will. All this gave him a thrill, motivated him, yet today there was nothing. Simply nothing.

He walked across the room and sat at his desk. From here he looked out across the city, two glass walls with nothing to obscure the view, yet he saw nothing. He swung round to his desk. What was happening? He was always so confident in all that he did. His father had taught him well, he was driven. Driven to such an extent that he had no time for anything else. His business and its expansion was all he thought about.

His eyes fell on the wooden sculpture his mother had left him. A parting gift. He remembered their last dinner together; he had enjoyed it, he had even relaxed. It had seemed that she had a new lease of life. The fact that she had gone on a holiday was amazing, that she had retired was even more so. When he had asked why she had simply said 'It is time', and had left it in the air, no other comment, just 'It is time'. Yet he had a feeling that there was more to her words than she was telling him. Then a week later the family lawyer had called him to tell him that his mother had instructed him to sell her house. Just what was she doing? Was this unexpected behaviour of his mother affecting him? He didn't like mysteries; he liked everything in black and white, grey didn't exist for him and the change in his mother was definitely a grey area. Grey areas he had no control over. No, it wasn't his mother, it was something else affecting him, but what?

He touched the wood and he felt it again, a connection. He felt something he couldn't quite define, but it felt quite peaceful. It was a memory almost, a memory that passed before his eyes but he couldn't quite grasp it. Just like trying to remember a name, you could see it yet couldn't read it. It was frustrating. He wondered where his mother was now, he hadn't heard from her since she had left New York. He thought about her decision to sell her home and he felt drawn to it. He walked out of his office, told his shocked secretary to cancel all appointments for the day and drove to his mother's house. Always his mother's house, never home.

He stood there in the hallway and the memories of his childhood returned and with them their pain. The cruel rejection by his father. The obvious favouritism his father showed towards his sister. Never for James the spontaneity of his sister towards their father. He was not allowed to interrupt the great man when in his study. It was he who was so often reprimanded. He who was excluded. His father would often have a business meeting when it was his school sports day, or when he played in little league. Yet he was always available for his daughter's events. James never resented Silvie; he loved her unconditionally. Yet he had never understood why his father treated his children so differently. James had learnt to hide his feelings, to adjust to what his father had expected of him. He had learnt not to trust his feelings other than the negative feelings. He had learned his father's ways; so well had he done this he had turned into his father. He had closed down and in doing so had lost himself. He thought about this; if he had lost himself then who was he? What was he doing here, why was he reliving these painful memories, why now? What the hell is going on? He felt as though he was losing control, he must be in control. Why? came the thought. He felt inexplicably exhausted. He walked into the living room and lay down on the settee and fell into a deep sleep.

He sat bolt upright, where was he? It was dusk and he suddenly remembered where he was. He had been dreaming, he had been peaceful, content but he didn't remember the dream, only the feelings that came with it and suddenly the words 'It is time'. He sat there trying to remember more, yes trees he remembered trees but nothing else. 'It is time', he had heard these words before, but where? Yes that's what his mother had said to him. He must have been dreaming about her, her holiday and her words, yes that was it. He was in control again, no grey area, no mystery. But he had a nagging suspicion that it was something else. He chose to ignore this. On his journey home he thought about work and the day ahead. He dismissed his visit to the house.

He had a breakfast meeting the following day, yet he was distracted throughout. He returned to his office, yet he couldn't keep his mind on his work. Try as he might he found himself day dreaming but never knowing what he was day dreaming about. His colleagues noticed the change in him and they too wondered what was happening. By lunch James decided to again cancel his appointments and left the office. He had no idea as to what was happening to him. Those words kept coming back to him 'It is time'. But time for what?

He went home to his apartment, the penthouse. Understated opulence. He stood in there looking at his home, yet it wasn't a home. His dissatisfaction returned. 'What the bloody hell is happening to me?' He walked out and went for an uncharacteristic walk and soon got lost. He realised he knew nothing of the area other than what he saw from his car. He walked on, he needed to expend his pent up energy, he needed to walk off this anger that was rising within him. The anger that he had suppressed for so many, many years. The years he had smothered his feelings, the years he had been buried. He walked. He wasn't even aware of his surroundings. He walked for hours, no thoughts in his head, only the relentless walking. Finally he found himself in a park and sat down exhausted on a bench. He looked around him. There were trees, trees? Trees again, he remembered them from his dream yesterday, nothing else, just the trees. He didn't understand. He didn't understand the trees, the loss of the thrill of business, the thrill even he had each time he returned home and saw his apartment. He didn't even seem to care about the business or his 'home'. He had lost something and was confused. He sat there in his confusion when the words again came to his mind 'It is time'. And for the first time in his adult life he felt defeated. He felt himself falling down into a big black hole. It was unfamiliar to him, he was out of control and he couldn't do anything about it. He didn't even want to, he just wanted it all to go away and leave him alone. But what did he want to go away? He just didn't know.

He sat there for a long time, the feelings sweeping over him, the pain of rejection by his father, the knowing he didn't really count until he proved himself in business. He had adapted himself to become his father, he even laughed like him and he hated himself for it and the hole became darker and deeper. He had lost who he was. Had he ever been allowed to be who he was? Yes he had, in his early years with his mother, yet in wanting his father's love and approval, he had even rejected her. Deeper he went. And in the black hole he fell asleep.

He dreamt of a young boy, a boy in tune with nature. A boy running in the fields, along the beach, building sandcastles with his mother. His mother always there, answering his questions, loving him, being with him, his one constant. He saw this young boy come to him and comfort him in this deep dark hole. The young boy had been waiting for him; he had held his memories for him, ready to return them to him for his healing. He told him it was OK to be who he really was. He didn't have to conform, he wasn't born for that. He was born for something else. It is time. It is time to let go. It is time to begin. The end is here. The beginning is here. It is time. I am with you. Join me. And in his dream he joined the boy, he became the boy. He became himself.

John finished loading his truck. Looking at the number of pieces he had loaded he realised it had been some time since he had last visited the gallery. It was a long journey and he set off early. He always looked forward to the drive, he found it relaxing. It was a mini holiday in fact. It was his time to get into contact with the outside world. He loved his life, he loved the remoteness of the valley, the mountains, no telephone, no TV and no radio. Yes he loved being alone, here in this special valley. Yet he was never alone, he felt as though the valley spoke to him. It gave him peace when he needed it. It comforted him in the times he felt the loneliness of his life and it had given him so much more. It had given him back those four days. The four days he had made himself forget because they always brought with them the pain of her leaving. But now he remembered them without any pain, yes there was the longing for her, that would always be there. But he knew they would meet again, if not in this life then the next. They were destined to be together throughout time.

Without the gift of those four days and the pain that followed he would not be doing what he was doing now, delivering his sculptures to the gallery. After she left he could not face the world, he could not take up the job that was waiting for him, he withdrew. In doing so he found solace in the pieces of wood that he found. He lost himself in the process of rubbing them down until they became smooth and tactile. He suddenly saw that the wood had given him so much. The wood had healed him. The process of working with each piece had slowly brought him back to life. Yes, he had buried the memory, but in doing so he had moved forward and found a love of each piece of wood and in doing so a greater respect for the valley and all it held.

He had understood his parents' fierce protection of it. He understood now that they had waited for him to accept responsibility of protecting the valley, of his love for it. Once he had done this their work was done and they had left the valley they so loved.

They had walked to their favourite place, a place that overlooked the valley and there they had let go of this life and returned home. John had found them there, locked together in an embrace, looking across the valley, the river that ran through it, the turquoise lake where they had taught him to swim and of the mountains that overlooked all. He had buried them there and often visited them. He talked to them, he told them of the changes with each season, he told them of the success of his sculptures, of how it enabled him to buy further pieces of land to expand the valley. And he felt their presence too. They were never far away from him. Always supporting him. Yesterday he had finally told them about Sarah, and in speaking out loud it had furthered his healing. He had wanted them to know but in talking it would have brought back the memories of the pain. So he had buried it. It was as though he had put the final piece of the puzzle in place. The healing was complete.

He had dreamt of her last night, she had called to him and he had gone to her. It was as if they had never parted. These memories brought a smile to his face. His was a handsome face, one on which his ancestors had left their mark. His dark black eyes, the blackness of his hair that he kept long in the traditional way. He felt it blowing in the wind from the open window, he felt good, so much he had let go of. Yes this was a new beginning. He felt something good was going to happen, an underlying excitement. He hadn't felt this way and this good for years. He laughed, last night's dream had done him good!

He drove into the town and pulled up outside of the gallery. The owner greeted him, he always felt the pleasure of meeting John again. He helped him unload and unwrapped each piece. He felt it, the strange connection, with what he didn't know, only that it gave him peace. It was a presence that seemed to fill the gallery. They talked, he offered John coffee, but he declined. One thing John always promised himself on these journeys was a meal and coffee at the diner down the street. He said his farewell and turned to leave. It was then the gallery owner remember the woman. He told John about her, that she was interested in meeting him. John felt the excitement stirring within him, and then he was given her name, Sarah. No it couldn't be, it just couldn't be. He was told that she was staying at the hotel at the end of the block. John turned and ran to the hotel. She wasn't there. Apparently she had taken to walking each morning, he followed the direction they told him she had taken. She had been gone for two hours, she must be returning soon. He caught his breath, he hadn't realised he was forgetting to breathe. It couldn't be her, but.......

As he walked into the woods at the edge of town he slowed his breathing, he stilled himself. Which way will I find her? He knew deep, deep down that it was her, why else had she come to him in his dreams, why now? He knew instinctively the path to follow and there she was walking towards him. The years fell away, it was just like the first time, he stood still watching her. Her head was down. Suddenly she looked up and saw him standing there, with his gentle smile. She knew he had been watching her. She stood still. Is it really him? She had wanted him for so long she thought she was imagining him. He said simply, 'Hello Sarah' and she knew. They ran to each other and time stood still. They were hungry for each other, he kissed her face, her eyes, her neck. Their passion was so great that it overwhelmed them, they surrendered themselves to it there on that woodland pathway. It was as if the years had fallen away. There was no shyness, no doubt. He still wanted her, she had returned to him. The talking would come, now was a time to release the pain of parting, a time to cross the bridge of time, a time to release all of the pent up emotions of being apart for all of these years. A time to take themselves to that other world, that other plain, and they reached it together. The spasms ran through their bodies, they were one. They lay in each others arms looking up at the trees above them. The sunlight shining through creating the dappled light that bathed them, a gentle breeze caressed their wet bodies. They were spent, it had all been let go. They were together again and each knew they would never part again. No words had been spoken, there was no breath for them. They kissed and in doing so they broke the spell. Slowly they dressed and left the woods, their arms around each other. Neither could bear to let go of the other, neither could bear to be separate from the other and both wanted only to feel the other's touch. They were home.

They returned to her room; they needed privacy, they were not ready to share each other with the world outside. And so in the privacy of her room they talked. They talked of the pain of their separation, of the lives they had lived, of her husband's death, her unhappiness in her marriage and about his sculptures she had found and the dreams she had had of him. And the journey they had led her to take and finally she told him of her one secret that she had kept all of these years. A secret she knew she must keep even as she left him all those years ago; she told him about his son. The son who had been born with his father's eyes, his father's gentle face and the son she had lost to her husband.

John sat there in silence, he had felt her pain of the years of an unhappy marriage. But he found it difficult to register what she had just told him. He had a son, a son he knew nothing of, a son he had not even met, yet alone held as a babe. He had a son; he should be angry with her for not telling him, but strangely he wasn't. She had borne this alone, without his support. He always believed that things happen for a reason but this was shaking that belief. He had a son, a grown son. He was a part of him and he ached for him. Then she showed him the photograph, it was him at that age, yes he was his son, their resemblance was uncanny. She had borne his son. He sat there stunned, silent.

She had told him too soon, she had lost him. He just sat there, he didn't say anything. She should never have kept it from him, but she didn't even know his name, there was no way to trace him, she knew of his life but not specific details. She told him this, she pleaded with him to speak. Her pleading brought him back. He took her in his arms and held her as she wept. He wiped away her tears with his kisses. He told her he loved her, that all was as it should be and that he would like to meet his son. He told her not to be sad and with his acceptance she sobbed.

She let out all of the unhappiness, all of the sadness of the past years of keeping this secret to her and her alone. She knew she was home and that all was well.

As her tears subsided he kissed her, and lifted her to the bed and made love to her. It was a gentle lovemaking. He poured all of his love into it and in doing so he took from her her pain, her unhappiness and her sadness. Then they fell into a deep sleep, entwined in each other.

He took her home to the valley. The minute they entered it she felt it. It had its own energy; it took her and held her. This is where she belonged. As she got out of the truck and stepped onto the land for the first time the words whispered themselves from her lips 'It is time'. He heard her and asked her to repeat them, she did and she knew that he knew the words too. But neither knew what they meant. Over the days that followed they realised that they had shared dreams, dreams that neither could quite capture but each remembered the feelings and the sensing of each other's presence. But always they remembered the words 'It is time'

They revelled in being together. He took her all through the valley. They camped by the side of streams. At night they lay looking up at the sky, so many stars. The moon watching over them. They made love in the moonlight. Theirs was a world at the exclusion of all else. The peace of the valley washed over them both and they forgot the past and lived in the present. They shared the beauty of this enchanted valley. Yes enchanted, that was the only word for it. He took her to the lake and they swam naked together, each feeling cleansed by its blue, green waters. Yet he couldn't find the glade and he knew instinctively that it was not time for her to go there. Not yet. The time is coming.

The weeks went by and it was as though they had been together for ever. They never wanted to be apart again. He told her about the family story and she felt a connection with it. She told him this but didn't understand it. He told her she would and then wondered where the words had come from. They looked at each other and laughed. There had been a lot of that going on, even in their shared dreams. Each knew something was happening that was leading them somewhere and it was going to happen soon.

They returned from one of their trips into the valley to find a car outside the house. No one really came there and neither recognised the car. There was no one to be seen and they assumed the visitor was in the house as it was never locked. They walked in without any fear, but both came to a standstill as they saw who the visitor was.

James stood up as they walked in. He saw the surprise on his mother's face. A face now without the lines of the last years. A face that was animated, open and loved. The face of the man was also surprised, yet it was a familiar face, a kind and gentle face, a face to be trusted. As they had walked in they had looked happy together as though they belonged together. Comfortable, like well-loved old sweaters.

Sarah looked at James and saw that he had changed. She walked to him and held him in her arms, something that he rarely allowed her to do, yet today he welcomed the hug, he even returned it. She felt the child in him coming home. Not a needy child, but one who gave freely, one who could also comfort, yet not a child. Gone was the hardness of the past years, back was the gentle soul of his early childhood. She was overwhelmed with the love she felt for her son, she thought she had lost him, that he had lost himself, but he was here and he was back. What had brought about this change she had no idea. She saw and was grateful for the change in him. She held him at arms length and looked into his eyes. She saw they sparkled, they had life in them again. No longer the gaunt features, the hardness. Gone was the armour he had protected himself with all of these years. He was open again, yet it had only been a few months since she had last seen him. How had this change come about? She wouldn't ask, she would wait until he chose to tell her.

James too felt as though he had come home, these past months had been difficult for him. He hadn't known why the things that happened to him were happening, only that he eventually surrendered to them. His brilliant analytical mind was of no use to him these past weeks. He simply understood that something was happening and he let it happen. It is time; the recurring theme that continually came to his mind, it is time. What it is he had no idea, he only knew that he was in some way being led forward. His instincts told him to listen to his thoughts. Thoughts that he knew were not his, at first he thought he was going mad, but the more he surrendered the more relaxed he became. In surrendering he came to the peace that had, for all his life, eluded him. He had been led here. He knew he had to find his mother and he had, here she was. She was a part of what was happening to him; so too was this stranger she was with. A stranger that she looked so happy with. A man standing back, watching him and his mother. He knew instinctively that this was a man of integrity, a man of strength, no not just physical but a strength that came from deep within his soul, a man he wanted to know.

James stepped away from his mother and walked across the room to the man, he held out his hand and introduced himself. He was suddenly overwhelmed by the love that came to him from this stranger, yet he wasn't a stranger? Something within James told him something that he was shocked to hear, yet he wasn't surprised. He halted his progress towards him. Suddenly a very large piece of the jigsaw fitted into place. He turned and looked at his mother. She was glowing, he felt her unconditional love for him and he felt too the love that she had for this man. He knew then that this was an old love, not one of the last months, or even years but of lifetimes. Yes, even his thinking was changing. Two months ago such a thought would have been scorned and tossed aside, but now it was the most natural thing to him. He looked from his mother to this man and back again. It was as though they too could hear the same thought. It was as though they were silently telling him.There in that room, a room that he had immediately felt at home in when he had walked in only a few hours ago, a room full of love, he voiced his thought. And as he did so the thought took form and the form completed his homecoming. To him this stranger was no stranger, this was his father. He felt no anger, he felt no shock, he simply felt as though he had come home, home to this love that surrounded and enveloped the three of them. He walked up to his father and they held each other. One coming home and the other totally overwhelmed by the love that he felt for his son.

She watched the moving scene in front of her. She had wondered how she would tell James, how he would take the news that this was his father. That she had lived a lie for all of his life. She had fantasized his reaction, his violent temper. The temper that had erupted in his early years. Oh she remembered it so well. In his loneliness and rejection, his need for his father's love and approval he became angry. Never at another but always at objects. She too in her loneliness and unhappiness in what was now a loveless marriage had become angry. At times it just became too much to bear, she had adapted to keep the peace and in doing so had lived a lie. Was this then something her son had sensed? Her husband away from home so much on business, she tried to cope with her frustrated child. She knew he was in so much pain but she was unable to reach him. That at times his anger would be so great that she could not control herself either and she would hit him, not just once... It was as though her son wanted her rejection too. Two people with the same pain, hurting each other.

She had never forgiven herself for these moments, even now the memory of them brought shame to her. It was then she had decided she needed to move her children from the toxic environment they were living in. It was then that she had found them boarding schools. Sylvie took to it straight away, she loved the life. She had always felt loved, she loved the adventure, the new friendships. She had always been so open, the memories of her snuggling up to her, of her climbing on her knee for a cuddle, of their laughing together at certain programmes they both enjoyed on TV as she got older.

To James though it was evidence of further rejection, but as the first few months went by he relaxed into his new school. It wasn't a strict regime, the boys were allowed freedom. In the grounds there were woods, trees to climb, but most of all other boys with whom he cemented life long friendships. To James the masters became the fatherly figures he so badly needed. In finding the love and friendship at the school his temper abated. It was only at holiday time did his reserve and distance with both his parents surface. Often as a teenager he would be invited to have holidays with his friends. She saw less and less of him. Sylvie too as she became older seemed to avoid home as much as possible. Sarah had taken her solace in her work. Unable to reach either child, unable to ease their pain, unable to ease her own pain. But now it was as if all this had been washed clean.

This moment of father and son meeting for the first time, the love that surrounded them all, she felt more than before that this truly was a new beginning. No more secrets. Secrets, the bane of all families. Why oh why do we keep secrets? They all tended to come to the surface in some form or other eventually. Even to be acted out by future generations. It was there in their collective memories. If they were not addressed and laid to rest they sat there waiting. They waited until a time when someone strong enough would stop the cycle. Was this perhaps a part of James's earlier frustration, had he the knowledge that she was lying to him, keeping his parentage from him? That she too was living a lie that she was happy with his father. Children have an uncanny way of knowing. They could pick up the slightest nuance. They could not identify what it was, only that something didn't feel right. Children after all lived with their feelings, they didn't analyse as adults did. They lived in the moment and were in tune with themselves and others. Oh yes, we adults thought we could keep things from them, we even fooled ourselves by burying things deep inside ourselves, but they sensed them.

Had James known that she wasn't being straight with him and in knowing had this added to his frustration and anger without his realising why? Was this too why Sylvie, her precious Sylvie, had turned from her? Had she too seen the lie she had been leading, had she too seen that her mother had not been straight with her and in not being straight had lied to not only her children but most of all to herself?

Where did these thoughts come from? Now of all times. Now, when there was so much love here, only now did they surface. But these thoughts gave her an insight that she had never recognised before. It was as if it was time to finally lay to rest all of the pain of her life. She forgave herself then. It was then she began to truly love herself.

She looked at the two men in front of her, she was blessed, truly blessed. She didn't know what had happened to change her son, but she knew something had. She had both of her beloved children back and she had too the man she loved so dearly. Yes, blessed was the only word to describe how she felt.

She walked over to them and held them both and the tears gently fell, tears of happiness and joy.

James told them what had happened to him these past months, of what had brought him to them. Of his increasing dissatisfaction with his business, of his dreams that he could not quite remember, of the time in the park when he had sunk into a deep despair to be rescued from it by himself, his inner child. He told them too that he knew he must find his mother, that he must be where she was, this above all he knew he must do. Of how he had used a detective agency to find her. How he had handed the day to day running of the business to his stunned management team and walked away from it, and the liberation he felt in doing so. The knowing that he was being guided in some way. The knowing that he was doing what he was meant to do, whatever that was. That the answers would come. But most of all, and continually recurring, was the phrase 'It is time'.

John and Sarah looked at each other and then back at James. It is time. So James too had those words in his head. They then told him that they too had those words, that they didn't know either what they meant, only that they both knew that something was going to happen and soon. They had never expected James to appear. They had never expected what had happened tonight, yet it all seemed so right. They were not going to question it although they couldn't resist wondering what would happen next. It was as though they were living through something that was meant to be.

It was then that John's eyes fell on the photograph of his parents, he looked at his mother's face smiling at him and it was as though he had been struck by lightening; he physically jumped.

The others looked at him. He told James the family story, of how he had laughed at his mother's insistence that he remember it all. Of how, once they knew he would carry on the story to his own children and that he would continue to protect the valley, that they had left him to return home. But the story had still remained a story to him. What if it wasn't just a story? What if....

He sat there thinking about the story. There was something he had forgotten, something he knew was important, but like so much recently, it evaded him. So he did what his mother had taught him; he let go of the thought, he knew it would come back and he would remember.

He watched mother and son mending their bridges. She answered the questions he had never asked, questions that he no longer needed the answers to but in verbalising them they lost the power they had had over him all these years. She told him that his father never knew that James wasn't his. His colouring could easily have come from his mother. That ,yes, he was resented but only because he came too early for his father. His father needed to be in control, he planned everything down to the last detail. James had arrived two years early, he was not on plan and his father took it too personally. To him, having a baby was a burden, he was setting up his business, he needed his wife to entertain, not to be tied to a child. Yes he was a selfish man and a jealous one too. He could not understand the symbiotic love of a mother and child, he couldn't understand the joy that Sarah experienced at being with her child, of teaching him about the world he lived in. Not for him jumping in puddles, not for him gathering the leaves only to jump into them and disperse them all again by running through them and kicking them, not for him having his child snuggle up to him for a story. He hadn't had that in his life, he had been taught control by his strict father. He could not let go and enjoy being with his child. Sarah tried to help him but he rejected her efforts. He remained behind the wall he had built to protect himself from his own father, a wall that he kept in place all of his life. He was not a man to be hated, but one to be loved. In his own way he loved James, but just did not know how to show it. It was only when James showed an interest in the company that his father found a way of sharing himself with his son. But in doing this he had done to his son what his father had done to him. James too had built his own wall, but he had learned well; his wall had become his prison, his high security prison.

All that had now fallen away, their bridges had been mended and they had crossed them to meet the other. It was as though the years had fallen away. He could once again accept the love that was so freely given to him. In doing so he realised the pain his mother had been in all these years, how she had worked so hard at trying to give her children a happy life; but she had been working against the odds and had lost herself in the process. But not now; he saw his mother as she truly was. A woman who loved her children more than he would ever know. And in that loving she had let them go. Yet she was always there. It was only now that he could see the sacrifice she had made, how she had given up this man, his real father, for the other man in her life. But her life hadn't followed the path she thought it would, he could see that now. She said nothing of the unhappiness in her marriage; she didn't have to. The memories came back to him and he could see the life she had led. Yet now here she was, looking so happy, so young. This man, John, was the cause of all this. Yes she had returned to him, she had come home. So too had he and in doing so both had released the past. They fell silent and let the peace of this place wash over them.

It was then she told them of her second secret; no more secrets, no more secrets. She told them of the devastating news the doctors had given her just a few months ago. She saw the effect this had on both men. Even within the love that was in this room, she saw their pain, especially that of John. Both moved towards her, both opened their mouths to speak, but she stopped them. She told them that without that diagnosis she would not be here today, they would not be here together today. It was the diagnosis that had inspired her, motivated her. It was in her despair that she had found the gallery and in finding the gallery she had found John's wood. Without the wood she would not have found her way back to him. Neither would she have bought the second piece for James. Without the diagnosis she would not have been reconciled with both of her children. The diagnosis had been her new beginning. She was just realising this. Her cancer, she told them, was the catalyst to all that had happened. She had been living a lie. And in living the lie she had lost herself. In losing herself she had stopped living. Oh she went through the motions, she had all the money she needed to do what she had wanted to do, yet she had never known what she wanted for herself other than her work. So used had she been to pleasing others she had no idea of how to please herself. She had stagnated and, she now understood, she had begun a downward spiral.

Yes it was the cancer that had brought her round, the cancer that had led her to put her first step forward to finding herself again, the cancer had given her so much. She sat there as if in a dream, not speaking to them but simply speaking her thoughts as they came to her. Her cancer was not the life threatening disease the doctors had predicted. Her cancer was a warning. A warning from her body that she was living a lie, she could see it now, oh so clearly.

The day of the diagnosis she had felt the depths of despair; she could feel the pit opening up before her. Only John's wood stopped her as she neared the precipice. He had pulled her back from the edge. She had made decisions then that a week before she would never have dreamt of; she would have rejected them as ridiculous, preposterous even. Yet she gave up her job, her house. Her decision to find John had changed her life and the lives of her children. She knew then that the cancer was not her enemy but her friend. Without it she would not have the happiness and joy she now felt. She had ignored the other signs her body had sent her so it had decided to make her sit up and take notice. And ,oh boy, had she taken notice. No she would not die of the cancer and why not you may ask. She would not die because she was again doing what she was meant to do, she was not destined to die of this disease. This is what she was here to do, this is where she was meant to be. She thanked the cancer for giving her this. The cancer had brought her back onto her true path. Oh yes she had so much to thank it for. It was then a beatific smile crossed her face. In seeing this both men knew she was right. She came out of her trance and looked at them both. This is the beginning not the end, not even the beginning of the end, this is the beginning.

It was then that the memory came back to John and a smile spread across his face. The others looked at him and he told them the missing part of his family's story, the missing part that was pivotal to the story; the one thing the ancestors had told them never to forget. He told them that he knew now why they had each lived the lives they had lived. That they were following a predetermined path. That in letting go of their past they cleared the way forward to the end of the story. It IS time, he told them and he knew what they must do.

The ancients, he told them, had been given an artefact. They had secreted it inside a tree and it would be found by those destined to use it to save Mother Earth and mankind.

But he instinctively knew that the artefact in the tree was not an object, but the tree itself. He saw in his mind's eye that the tree had lived its life and as it grew it became a more powerful energy. That it put down roots which in turn put up shoots and became more trees. The shoots were a perfect circle around the tree. Each of the shoots was infused with the powerful energy of its mother tree and over the generations of trees, the circle grew ever wider and with it the energy. The area where the original tree had been planted, in what was now the centre of the circle, carried the knowledge and energy of the trees, and as each tree completed its time on earth it nourished the centre. This space, encircled by the trees, became the glade to which only John had been granted entry. It was from the glade that the work would begin with a ripple that would rapidly spread until the world was to become what it was always meant to be. All men would live at one with each other and the earth. As he saw it he told the others and they too saw it.

None of them understood what their role in all of this was. Only that they had been brought together for a reason and it had to do with the glade. He told them of his visits to this glade, of how it had healed him when he needed it, of how it gave him the answers when he needed them and of how he could never find it when he wanted to. The glade would guide him there when he needed it. It was as though it could sense him, as though it called him home to nurture him when he needed to be nurtured. He told them of its beauty, no matter the season, of the overwhelming feeling of peace and love that it gave to him. Yes, it all became so clear to him now. He knew too that the three of them would be led there when the time was right.

Suddenly they all heard it, they sat there stunned. The voice was no longer in their heads, it was as though someone else were in the room. They all heard it and they knew it to be true. 'It is time'. In hearing the voice they knew it was time to leave the cottage.

Dawn was breaking as they left the cottage. The forest canopy had not yet let the breaking light through but they had no difficulty in walking through the forest. Their path seemed to be illuminated. In the distance they could see a silvery blue ball of light that they knew was leading them forward. They had no fear of what they saw, they felt no surprise; it was natural to them, as though it were an everyday occurrence. Even as the sun rose in the sky their path was still illuminated, the ball of light continued to lead them forward.

They walked for several hours until they were led into the glade.

The light led them to the centre and they were told to rest. Each felt a tide of tiredness wash over them and they lay down and instantly fell asleep. With the sleep came the dream; they lived the family story. But it was no longer a story, they saw themselves as the original elders of their tribe. They had been together even then. The story unfolded before them. Their contented lives, the appearance of the white buffalo to them, its transformation into the woman dressed in white, her long blue black hair tied back; her message to them; the journey that they took to this sacred place; of the white buffalo woman's re-appearance to them; her gift to them of a tree that was to be planted here. They saw the generations that followed, generations who had lived and died until only three survived. They were those three. Sarah, until now, had no knowledge that her ancestry was linked to John's, many generations back but none the less still linked, They were the last three.

They were shown that all that had gone before was pre-destined, that each had lived their lives as they were meant to be.That each had fulfilled their purpose to be able to be here now. And only in fulfilling their purpose could they do what was to be done.

On waking they sat on the ground facing each other some distance apart. It felt so natural, so familiar. It was as though they had been transported back to being the original elders, the ancient ones. John found himself saying the sacred words, words he had never heard before, yet they came as no surprise. Each then focused their eyes on the centre of their circle, the point of their focus an old gnarled tree stump, barely visible amongst the grasses, the remains of the original gift from the white buffalo woman. As they focused they saw a pin prick of pure white light. The light expanded the more they focused on it. Then suddenly tiny multicoloured sparks of light shot out from it. These sparks surrounded them as they sat in wonder at what was unfolding before them. They held their concentration as each spark changed to a vertical beam of light. Each vertical beam of light then slowly took form. They recognised each form; they were their ancestors, all who had brought about the journey to this sacred valley, all those who had been the guardians of this sacred valley. They stood there behind the three of them, encircling them.

John's parents stood behind James, they smiled at John and he knew they knew all that had happened to him, that they gave him their blessing and love. Each of them, John, Sarah and James knew each of their ancestors; they didn't know how they knew, they didn't need to, they simply knew.

It was then that the three of them saw their previous selves, saw who they were in their previous lives, from when they were the ancient ones, the elders. Each of their previous selves came forward and sat beside them. They formed the inner circle within the outer circle of the sacred trees, with their ancestors forming circles in between. It was then that the ancient ones said 'It is time'. As these words were spoken each of them recognised the voices, the voices they had been hearing these past weeks, the voices that had led them here.

All there, in this magical glade, turned to the light that still glowed at the centre of all. This was what, over the centuries, they had been born to do, this was what the centuries had led them to do. All concentrated on the light and as they did it grew ever brighter. It began to change shape until it too became a beam of pure white light. The light and its energy grew and spread a canopy over the glade. The energy suddenly expanded as though it were a massive explosion, yet a silent one. Its mushroom cloud shot around the earth, a beam of amazing beauty and speed. It was a beam of love to light up the hearts of man. Its power was immeasurable. It held the fascinating, deadly beauty of an atomic explosion. But this was not a deadly energy; on the contrary, this was a life giving energy. This was an energy that would enter the hearts of every person on the Mother Earth. This was an energy that would touch all living things on Mother Earth and Mother Earth herself. This was an energy of such wonder that man did not have the imagination to comprehend it. Nor would man need to comprehend it. Man would have no knowledge of what was happening tonight. Only those present here knew, only those here tonight could see. But the hearts of all would change from this point on. This then was what they were here to do tonight, this was the beginning, of what, they did not know.

Suddenly the energy contracted; the canopy above them became a horizontal beam of light and this beam in turn became the ball of light. They saw their ancestors begin to fade. John saw for the last time his parents smile, the love in their eyes, as they too began to fade. Each turned once more into the tiny pin pricks of light and returned to the central ball of light. All with the exception of their previous selves.

They saw each of their previous selves merge with their ancient elder selves. Their elder selves spoke to them, yet although they heard the words, no words were spoken. Their elders then gave them another gift. They told them they had seen all who had gone before; they had been shown all that they had lived through to enable what had happened tonight. What they were then given was a brief view of the future. A future from which all that had happened in the past and tonight would lead to.

They saw a world where all were recognised for their own worth, with each seen as part of the whole. There would be no sickness as each would learn to go within to resolve any issues. Through the love of all sentient beings all would be loved; they could ask for and would be given all the help they needed. There would be no evil. From this point forward all sentient beings would begin to learn to live with each other. It would take time, but things would now change, slowly, very slowly at first. They saw how each of them would contribute to this changing earth. The more they were given the more they understood what they now were here to do. In understanding the pictures faded, but not the elders.

Suddenly the elders stood before each of them. They were to be given one last gift. This lifetime, they were told, was for all to remember. No books could give them what they already knew. To read books would not give the peoples of this earth what they were looking for. Only within were the answers and the knowledge to be found. They were now to be given the gift of remembering what they already knew. And as they heard these words each elder stepped forward and joined with them. And in doing so they remembered. They saw all that had gone before and all that was to come. They saw their pathway. They knew this was a sacred gift, that it was a gift that only they had been given, but the greatest part of this gift was the knowledge that each would no longer linger in their past. Neither would they live for their future. Each would live in the now. All peoples would only be able to follow their path by living in the now. In living in the now, moments would not be lost, people would not be ignored, each would be acknowledged. Love would grow. Love was the most important of all. Without love humans' hearts would not open; love had been given tonight. The love that was the first step in remembering, the first step in living from the heart.

They each then understood the lives they had led, the pathways they had followed, the pain they had each endured, their experiences. Each knew that their lives had been set out before they had been born, that they had been part of the planning of their lives. Yes, they had diverted from their paths but always they had returned. These diversions had often given them pain, but in time they had returned, guided; they saw that now. Never alone, always, always the love they had experienced tonight, always there. They had seen so many tonight; they too were there and they too had always been there. They could not see them now, but they felt their presence. So much love. It was this love that had taken them by the hand and had led them along their paths. It was this love that still held their hand when they wandered off their paths, a love that held them when they struggled, when they felt despair. This love that had sustained them, that had brought them through everything that had gone before and was there now and would continue to be with them in this life and beyond.

They had no fear of the future. They had seen the vision of the future, their futures, of the role they would each play in moving the peoples of the world towards this vision. A future where each man would be valued for who he is, not for what he possessed, not for the amount of money he had and not for his status. Money would not be required, each would attain their potential, each would have the joy of living and doing what made their heart sing and all would be done with love.

John saw that he would continue to work with the wood he was given by this valley, that he would work with the valley. He could now see how the valley had spoken to him for all of his life, yet he had never been aware of this, only of the energy it gave him, of how he felt at peace, of how it had healed his pain. Now though, he knew he would work with the valley, that it would expand, that it would give up its secrets to him and he would pass them on. That the great forests of the world would also be protected, that they too would work with the peoples of this earth as he and they learned the new way of living. John saw too that the healing he had found here was to be found anywhere in nature. But nature not governed by chemicals; nature had her own way of fertilising her land. Nature would show the way to balance the needs of man.

John saw that he would no longer be alone in this valley, that others would come. They would come to learn and they would take their learning home and spread the knowledge. John knew that Sarah would be there with him, that they would work together. He saw how compatible their work was for what was to be done. They had seen their future together and the generations to come and in this he found comfort. He had not realised the loneliness he had felt. If he had been told just a few weeks ago that others would come to the valley he would have hated the idea. Yet now he embraced it. He knew when they came they wouldn't know why they came. He knew that they would be guided, the valley would give them what they needed to take their next step forward. Their next step forward in remembering.

Sarah too saw that she would continue her work, but she would be here, here with John. She would learn the old ways from him. It would be she who would take the old and the best of the new and she would write about this valley and the ways to work with nature. But they wouldn't be the technical papers and books she had previously written; her new books would not be for a specialist market. She would write books that would guide people into living and working with nature. Her books would be written in this valley and the valley would not only be in the books but the spirit of the valley would be in the books too, just as the spirit of the valley was in each of John's pieces of wood. Her books would touch the hearts of those who read them.

And James knew now why he was here, why he had been born and brought up believing Jack to be his father. He was meant to be the head of the company his father had created, he was meant to expand it. He knew too the reason for his dissatisfaction, his restlessness that had brought him here. He knew what he was going to do, what he was meant to do. He smiled to himself and felt the peace within him. It all made sense to him now. It would take time, time was what he had. He was no longer alone, he felt their presence. He knew they would answer him when he spoke to them. The love would be there as it always had been. Strange he thought to himself, I have fought to find my way all of my life, when all I simply had to do was to be who I am. In being who

I am, in being true to me then I would have felt this peace, this knowing. But then I wouldn't have accomplished what I have done with the company. No more past, only the now and the future it would lead to. Again the smile spread across his face, a face so much younger now, a face at peace with itself.

They slept, a dreamless sleep this time. There would be time for talking, for reflection on what had happened tonight, but now they slept. There in the glade, watched over by the trees and nature, under a cloudless, star filled sky. They were where they belonged.

In the week that followed John took James into the valley. They walked the forest trails, camped and the son learned much from the father. They had a bond that would never be broken, not a new bond but one that had always been there, across all of their lifetimes. James knew the valley, he felt its familiar embrace; yes, he had come home. At the end of their journey through the valley John took his son to the lake; there they dived into its waters, the blue green waters that cleansed and energised them. Each knew then it was time to begin.

The three of them spent their last day together, they talked of what had happened there in the glade, of the vision of the future they had been given and the part each of them had in ensuring this future. They knew that there were others too working towards this future. That they would find each other and in doing so the love would grow. Each using the love to fulfill their lives, to follow their paths, in doing what they were meant to do, in doing what made their hearts sing.

John would continue to smooth the wood he was given by the valley; they knew now that these pieces had infused in them the spirit of the valley. A spirit that would touch the hardest of hearts, a spirit that would begin the changes in the hearts of men, a spirit that had always been connected to this valley, but had been strengthened by the beam that had shot around the world. Yes the spirit had begun to touch the people it was destined to help, but in strengthening it, each peace had become a beacon. Each piece would carry the love that man needed. Each piece would help man to remember.

James left the valley, and his parents. He had work to do, changes to make; he was fired up with enthusiasm, an enthusiasm he had never felt before. He would be gone from the valley for a long time. Already its beauty had become a part of him. He knew he would return, time and time again; he knew he would learn the ways of the valley from John, that each would take their place until he returned at last to stay. But that was a long way into the future. Today was the day he was to take his first step to that future. It was time for him to begin; it was time for the three of them to begin...

Acknowledgements

My thanks and love to my family
and friends for their encouragement and support.
To my scribe for his penmanship
and to my lovely husband Hans.

Thanks too to Lilian for her unfailing patience
and understanding each and every time I called her,
in my excitement, to read to her each and every section
after it was typed and to Lin for her gift of the title.